This book
belongs to

Walt Disney's
The Jungle Book

MOUSE WORKS

This is the story of Mowgli, the Man-cub who grew up in the jungle. He had many friends: the wolf family who raised him from a baby; Baloo, the happy-go-lucky bear who showed Mowgli how to enjoy life; the vultures who befriended him; and Bagheera the panther, who protected him. But the jungle is a dangerous place, and Mowgli had many enemies. There was Kaa, the python, who could hypnotize you just by looking into your eyes, and who would have liked to make a meal of the Man-cub. But Mowgli's greatest enemy, by far, was the fierce tiger, Shere Khan. He hated all men and swore that he would destroy the Man-cub before he could grow up.

This story begins long ago
when Bagheera, the panther,
first heard a strange sound
coming from a little broken
boat that had washed up on the
river's edge. It was the sound of
a baby crying. Bagheera looked
in the boat and saw a Man-cub
in a basket. Had he known how
deeply he was to become
involved, he might have obeyed his
first impulse and walked away.

Instead, Bagheera picked the basket up and considered
what to do with the baby. The Man-cub would need
nourishment—and soon. Then the panther remembered a
family of wolves that had been recently blessed with a litter
of cubs. He left the Man-cub basket at the entrance of the
wolf den and let them do the rest.

A little wolf cub discovered the basket first and sniffed at
the little stranger, saying, "What kind of cub is this?"

The baby boy stopped crying and smiled. Then the mother
wolf came close and sniffed him. He smiled again. And that's
how Mowgli found a family.

Ten times the rains had come and gone, and Bagheera often stopped by the wolf family's den to see how Mowgli was getting along. He was a favorite of all the wolf cubs. They grew and played together, and no son of Man was ever happier. And yet someday he would have to go back to his own kind.

One day Shere Khan, the tiger, learned about Mowgli. "A Man-cub living in the jungle with a pack of wolves," he growled to himself. "He may be harmless now, but he'll soon be a grown Man." Because Shere Khan hated all men, he decided to make sure that Mowgli would never grow up and learn to hunt. He started off in search of Mowgli and the wolf pack.

When the wolf pack learned that Shere Khan was looking for them, the elders called a meeting at Council Rock. The leader, Akela, was the first to speak: "Shere Khan will surely kill the boy and all who try to protect him. The boy can no longer stay with the pack."

"But Mowgli can't survive in the jungle alone," protested Rama, the Man-cub's wolf father.

Bagheera knew that Rama was right. Now it was up to him. He jumped down from a limb into the center of the gathering. "Perhaps I can be of help," he said to the startled pack. "I know a Man village where he'll be safe. I'll take him there myself."

And so it was decided. Mowgli was to leave for the Man village with Bagheera at once.

The panther tried to explain to Mowgli what had been decided and that they had to leave. There was no time to lose.

"No, I won't go," Mowgli sobbed. "I want to stay here with my mother and father. I don't see why I should go to a Man village. I want to live here in the jungle. It's my home."

Bagheera explained to him that the wolves still loved him, but because Shere Khan was hunting for him, everything had changed.

Mowgli held tight to a tree while Bagheera struggled to pull him away. Finally, he let go, and an unhappy Man-cub and a long-suffering panther were on their way.

Mowgli rode silently on Bagheera's back, and they went swiftly through the jungle. He was so quiet that Bagheera finally asked him, "Are you sulking?"

"No, not sulking, just thinking," Mowgli replied. "And I'm not scared of Shere Khan."

"Perhaps you aren't," Bagheera answered, "but you should be. He is a dangerous enemy."

Night was falling when
Bagheera finally stopped in
front of a big tree and helped
Mowgli climb up onto a high
branch. He was very tired and
didn't argue. He snuggled up
against Bagheera and they both
fell fast asleep.

But they were not alone. Kaa, the python, was hiding in the same tree.

"Is that a Man-cub I s-s-see?" he hissed, pushing his head down through the leaves.

Mowgli woke up to find himself face to face with the snake, looking into two big, round, yellow eyes that were staring right at him. "Go away, snake!" he shouted, staring right back into Kaa's eyes.

That's just what he shouldn't
have done. "I don't trust you,"
Mowgli said, beginning to get
dizzy.

"You can tru-s-st me,"
hissed Kaa. "I am your friend."
He continued to stare right into
Mowgli's eyes, and the Man-
cub couldn't look away. He was
under Kaa's spell.

Kaa wrapped his long tail around Mowgli. Still, Mowgli couldn't take his eyes off Kaa. Now he was helpless and couldn't move.

"Now I have you! What a good s-s-supper!" said Kaa,
opening his big jaws. Luckily his speech awakened Bagheera.
Seeing Kaa's open mouth heading for Mowgli made him
furious. He aimed a powerful blow right at the snake's jaw.
Whack! The stunned snake fell to the ground with a thud and
slithered away, muttering to himself.

"I hope that will teach you a lesson," Bagheera grumbled after him.

Then he turned to Mowgli and said, "Tonight Kaa tried to get you. Tomorrow it might be Shere Khan. You are not safe in the jungle any more. You must go to the Man village."

Mowgli was silent.

The next morning the two were awakened by a terrible
thundering, crashing noise.

"Keep it up. Hup! Two! Three! Four!" a deep voice
bellowed. Trees and branches crashed and the jungle shook.

"Oh, no," Bagheera groaned. "It's Hathi's dawn patrol."

Mowgli grabbed a vine and swung down to the ground for a closer look as a huge troop of elephants marched by.

Leading the way was Hathi, a big bull elephant shouting orders. The rest of the elephants followed in a line, trumpeting a military march.

The whole troop stamped along the path in front of
Mowgli, then turned and marched another way. This time
Mowgli turned with them and fell in line with a baby
elephant.

"Hello!" Mowgli said. "What are you doing?"

"Drilling," answered the little elephant. "SSSHHH! No talking in the ranks."

Mowgli followed the troop.
He marched on, stopped,
turned and changed direction,
all at Colonel Hathi's
command. But he forgot to
change direction once and
found himself face to face with
the baby elephant.

"Go the other way. Turn
around," coached his friend.

Mowgli turned and started
off in the other direction.

This was great fun. They marched and turned; then they turned and marched. Mowgli followed all of Colonel Hathi's orders.

"Living with an elephant herd would be a lot better than staying in a Man village," thought Mowgli.

Just when Mowgli was sure he had the knack of military drilling,
Colonel Hathi called for a stop.

"Ho! Company halt!" he bellowed.

The line of elephants came to an abrupt stop, one on top of the other.

"I'm putting in for a transfer," said one elephant. "My feet are killing me."

"Silence in the ranks," bellowed Colonel Hathi.

"What kind of soldiers are you?" he shouted. "Dress up that line!" All the elephants tried to stand as tall as they could in a straight line. The colonel looked them over. Then he called for an inspection.

"What's an inspection?" asked Mowgli.

"You'll see," said the baby elephant.

Mowgli watched all the elephants as they stuck their trunks up into the air and stood at attention. The baby elephant stuck his trunk up, too.

"Stick your trunk up," he whispered to Mowgli.

Mowgli pointed his nose in the air. "Like this?" he asked.

"That's right," said his friend.

The Colonel started down
the line of elephants with their
trunks pointed to the sky like
trumpets. He stepped in front
of one elephant and looked
down into his trunk. "Tsk, Tsk!
Tsk! What's this? A dusty muzzle.
That trunk can save your life.
You'd better take care of it," he
scolded.

He continued down the line,
inspecting trunks. Mowgli
stood very straight and tall,
trying to make up for not
having a trunk.

When Colonel Hathi got to
the little elephant, he looked
down and said, "Keep those
heels together, shall we, Son?"

"Right, Pop," answered the
baby.

33

"Well," snorted Colonel Hathi as he looked down at Mowgli. "What have we here? A new recruit?" Before Mowgli knew it, he was eye to eye with the big elephant, who was holding him up for a close inspection.

"Why, it's a Man-cub," he gasped. "And what, may I ask, are you doing here? There will be no Man-cubs in *my* jungle."

"It's not *your* jungle," Mowgli blurted out. He was furious and ready to make trouble. Bagheera quickly intervened.

"Hold it, hold it," he said. "I can explain. I'm taking the Man-cub to the Man village."

"To stay?" asked Colonel Hathi.

"Yes," Bagheera said. "You have the word of Bagheera."

With that, the Colonel released Mowgli, and they were on their way again.

Bagheera scolded Mowgli. "You were lucky I arrived when I did," said the panther.

"I would have managed. I can take care of myself!" Mowgli replied.

"That's what you think," Bagheera said. "You do have friends in the jungle, but you also have many enemies."

Mowgli was tired of listening to the panther remind him of the dangers, so Bagheera let him be by himself for a bit.

That proved to be a big mistake. For while Mowgli was moping around, a big, happy bear came by. It was Baloo.

Mowgli and Baloo quickly became friends. "Stick with me, kid. I'll teach you how to survive in the jungle," said Baloo after hearing Mowgli's story. "You won't have to go to the Man village."

The first thing Baloo taught Mowgli was how to growl like a bear.

Then Baloo taught Mowgli how to walk like a bear. He
even showed him how to scratch like a bear.

"How am I doing?" asked Mowgli.

"You'll make a great bear!" said Baloo.

Mowgli climbed up onto his back and said, "I like
traveling with you much better than with Bagheera. He's
always telling me what to do."

Baloo's next lesson on living in the jungle was how to find food. Both of them were hungry.

"There's lots to eat in the jungle," coached Baloo. "You just need to know where to find it." He showed Mowgli how to pick fruit off a prickly plant without getting stuck by the spines. It tasted good.

Then he showed Mowgli how to get honey from the bees
and bananas from the trees. "I'll teach you everything I know
about living in the jungle," said Baloo. "It's not so hard, once
you know how to find the bare necessities."

After a good meal, Baloo and Mowgli sang and danced through the jungle. They turned, jumped and spun around. Mowgli was very happy that he'd met Baloo. He was sure he could learn to survive on his own once Baloo showed him how.

They sat down together to catch their breath. A few minutes later Baloo asked, "What about a boxing match?"

"Great!" said Mowgli. He punched Baloo as hard as he could.

"Stop," protested Baloo, pretending to be hurt. "You win."

"You see," Mowgli said, "I *can* take care of myself."

"Sure ya can, Little Britches," grinned Baloo. "You're gonna make a great bear." He hoisted Mowgli on his shoulders, and they started down the path.

"Not so fast," Bagheera said. "I'm taking that Man-cub to
the Man village."

"You can't take him to the Man village," Baloo protested.
"They'll make a Man out of him."

"I want to stay here with you," wailed Mowgli, holding on
to Baloo.

"Nonsense," Bagheera said. He jumped onto a tree limb so he could look Baloo in the eye. "Shere Khan is nearby, looking for Mowgli. The Man-cub must come with me now."

Baloo gave the panther's tail a yank. "He's coming with me," he growled.

"Oh, very well. I give up. Hope your luck holds out," Bagheera called as Baloo and Mowgli continued down the forest path toward the river.

When they came to the river, Baloo jumped in and floated along on his back, with Mowgli riding on top of his big stomach.

"I want to stay with you forever," said Mowgli.

"You can, Little Britches," said Baloo. "I'll take good care of you, too."

Up in the trees along the river bank, the monkeys were chattering, but Mowgli and Baloo didn't notice. Baloo closed his eyes and started to sing.

After Baloo finished his song, he opened his eyes, only to find a monkey sitting on his chest instead of Mowgli.

"Where's Little Britches?" he cried. When he looked up, he saw that the monkeys had taken Mowgli and were holding him by the feet.

"Hey, let go of me!" called Mowgli as they dangled him overhead.

Baloo struggled upright in the water and shook his fist up at the monkeys. "Give me back my Man-cub," he yelled.

The monkeys laughed and chattered. This made Baloo even
madder. Then they dangled Mowgli down next to Baloo—just
out of reach. Baloo made a mad swipe, trying to grab Mowgli
away, but the monkeys were too fast. They pulled the Man-
cub away at the last second and disappeared in the trees
overhead.

Baloo got out of the water and chased the monkeys as they swung from tree to tree, holding tight to their captive. They passed Mowgli back and forth like a ball. Baloo could do nothing to stop them. While he looked up at the trees and raced through the jungle, two of the monkeys stopped long enough to trip him with a vine. The big bear fell with a thud, and the monkeys bore Mowgli away.

When Bagheera caught up to
Baloo, he said, "Well, it's
finally happened. It took a little
longer than I thought, but it's
finally happened."

Baloo looked at him with a
sad, dazed look on his face.
"What happened?" he said.
"Where's Mowgli?"

Bagheera told him that he
suspected the monkeys had
taken Mowgli to their king in
the old ruined city. And
Bagheera told him that they had
to go there at once. For the first
time in his life, Baloo listened
to him.

Bagheera was right. The monkeys had taken Mowgli to their leader, King Louie.

King Louie scratched his head and said, "So you are the Man-cub. Tell me the secret of Man's fire."

Mowgli insisted he didn't know the secret, but King Louie wouldn't believe him. He picked up Mowgli and swung him around. The other monkeys all took turns doing the same, until Mowgli began to feel a little dizzy. Soon the whole monkey troop was dancing around the old ruins.

While all this was going on, Bagheera was hiding, waiting
for the best time to jump out and snatch Mowgli away.

When everybody started dancing, a big monkey joined the
party. The big monkey was really Baloo. He had disguised
himself. No one but Mowgli recognized him.

Baloo started dancing, and all the monkeys followed him, clapping their hands.

King Louie was having a wonderful time. He clapped in rhythm, faster and faster. Suddenly, Baloo's coconut snout fell off, and the monkeys recognized him. "Baloo, the bear!" they all shouted.

Baloo grabbed Mowgli. The king did the same and they
both pulled Mowgli back and forth. Finally King Louie
tightened his grip on the Man-cub and braced himself against
one of the ancient columns—until it began to crumble. Then
there was a terrible creaking noise as the whole temple began
to collapse.

The king let go of Mowgli and rushed over to hold up the temple roof. Baloo let Mowgli go, too. Mowgli ran to Bagheera and Baloo rushed back to hold up the other crumbling pillar. Then a fiendish look crossed his face.

Baloo had an idea. He rushed over and started to tickle King Louie. It's not easy to hold a temple on your shoulders when someone is tickling you. King Louie let go of the temple roof just as Baloo ducked out, and the ruin began to sag and crumble around him.

When they reached a safe place to spend the night, Mowgli went right to sleep. Bagheera took the opportunity to talk to Baloo and finally convinced him that the Man-cub would be better off in the Man village. "It's up to you now," Bagheera told him.

"Why me?" said Baloo.

"Because he won't listen to me."

But when Baloo tried to explain all this to Mowgli in the morning, the Man-cub shouted, "You're just like Bagheera. I won't go to the Man village with you, either." And he ran off into the jungle.

When he was sure no one had followed him, he plopped down beneath a tree. The next thing he knew, he had been hoisted up onto a limb by the tail of the python, Kaa.

"S-s-so nice to s-s-see you again," hissed Kaa, bringing Mowgli up close to his face.

"Leave me alone," snapped Mowgli as he shoved the snake's head away. "And besides, I'm not looking into your eyes again. I know what you're trying to do."

"Oh, let me look at you," said Kaa. "I can help you stay in the jungle forever."

"You can?" asked Mowgli.

"I can," said Kaa. "Tru-s-st me. Just shut your eyes-s-s."

Mowgli's eyelids seemed very heavy, and they soon began to close. As Mowgli fell into a deep sleep, Kaa began to coil his body around the boy.

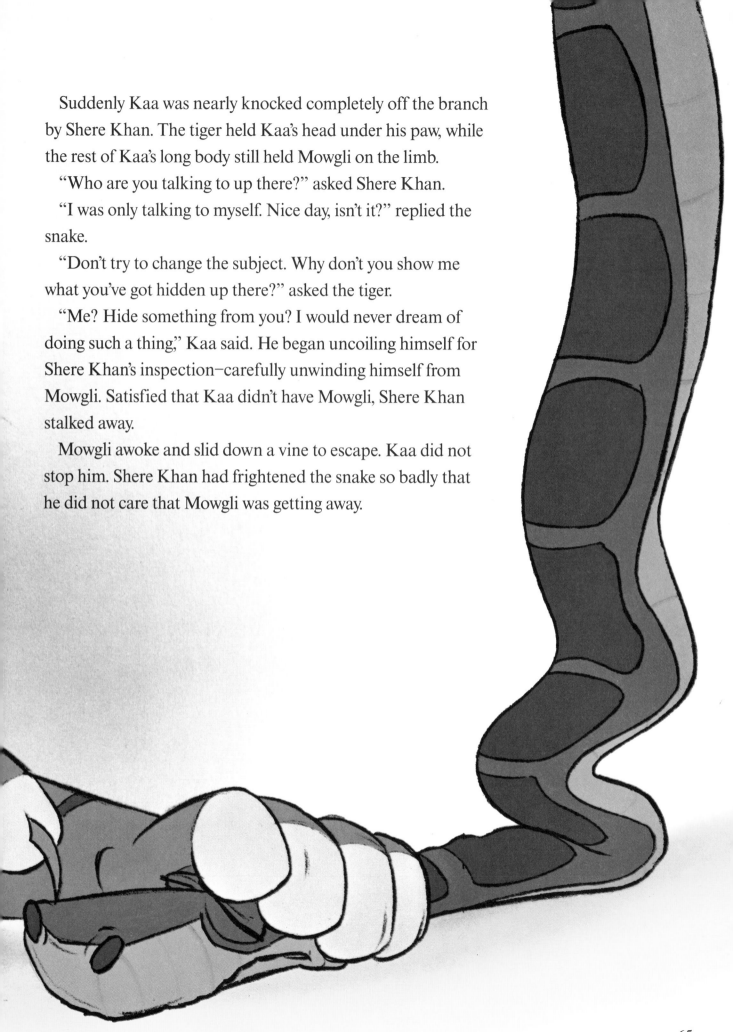

Suddenly Kaa was nearly knocked completely off the branch by Shere Khan. The tiger held Kaa's head under his paw, while the rest of Kaa's long body still held Mowgli on the limb.

"Who are you talking to up there?" asked Shere Khan.

"I was only talking to myself. Nice day, isn't it?" replied the snake.

"Don't try to change the subject. Why don't you show me what you've got hidden up there?" asked the tiger.

"Me? Hide something from you? I would never dream of doing such a thing," Kaa said. He began uncoiling himself for Shere Khan's inspection—carefully unwinding himself from Mowgli. Satisfied that Kaa didn't have Mowgli, Shere Khan stalked away.

Mowgli awoke and slid down a vine to escape. Kaa did not stop him. Shere Khan had frightened the snake so badly that he did not care that Mowgli was getting away.

Mowgli ran as fast and as far away as he could. It was late afternoon when he met a flock of vultures.

"Hold it, lads," said one of the vultures. "Look what's coming our way."

"What a crazy-looking bunch of bones," said another, and they all laughed.

"Go ahead and laugh," said Mowgli. "I don't care." And he climbed up on a rock and put his head down on his knees.

"Hey, now, kid," said one of the vultures. "Wait a minute."

"You look like you haven't got a friend in the world," said another vulture.

"We'll be your friends," they all said at once. The biggest vulture laid a wing across Mowgli's shoulders and they started to sing him a song about friends.

The vultures began to dance around Mowgli, cheering him up. He sang with them, and before long he was feeling much better.

"The jungle isn't such a dangerous place after all," thought Mowgli. "There are friends everywhere." Thinking of friends brought Baloo and Bagheera to mind, and Mowgli felt a pang of guilt. He hoped they weren't worrying about him, but he had little time to ponder, because suddenly a tremendous roar split the air.

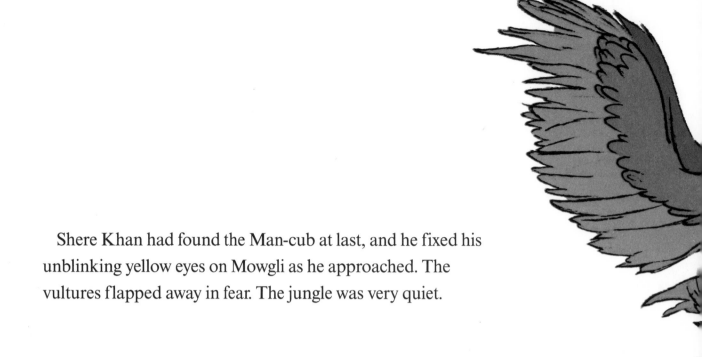

Shere Khan had found the Man-cub at last, and he fixed his unblinking yellow eyes on Mowgli as he approached. The vultures flapped away in fear. The jungle was very quiet.

Mowgli found himself face to face with his fierce enemy.

"Run! Run!" chorused the vultures as they circled above.

Mowgli was very scared, but he tried not to show his fear. He summoned his courage and said, "I am not afraid of you."

"You must be afraid of me," said Shere Khan. "Everyone is afraid of me."

"Well, I'm not!" said Mowgli.

"Look!" said the tiger. "I will count to ten and you try to get away." Then the tiger began to count, "One, two, three, four..."

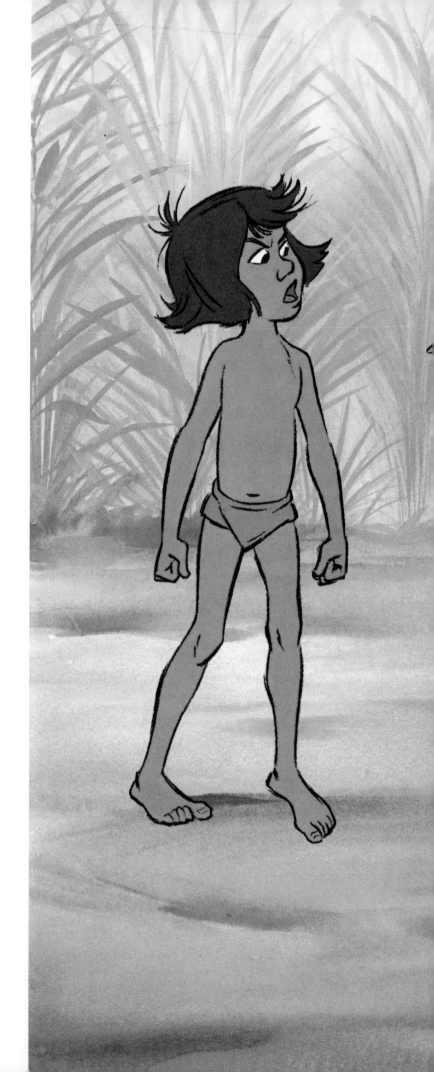

73

"Get ready, Mowgli!"
shouted one vulture.
"Run! Run, quickly!" said
another.
But Mowgli knew that
it was no use. Shere Khan
could run faster. If he ran he
would surely get caught.

Instead, he grabbed a branch and decided to fight, even if
he didn't stand much of a chance against Shere Khan. The tiger,
furious to see a tiny Man-cub stand up to him, gave a loud
roar and bared his sharp claws.

The tiger crouched, ready to pounce. But just as he leaped,
Baloo stepped out of the bushes. The big bear jumped in front
of the angry tiger and held his huge paw up in front of Shere
Khan, shouting, "Leave the Man-cub alone!"

"Out of the way," snarled Shere Khan as he rushed by.

Baloo did the only thing he could do. He grabbed the tiger by his tail.

"Run, Mowgli! Run!" Baloo yelled.

Mowgli started running, the tiger so close behind he could feel his hot breath on the back of his neck.

Baloo was pulled along behind the snarling tiger and the strategy worked. It slowed down Shere Khan enough so that he couldn't catch Mowgli.

The vultures flew to Mowgli's rescue and carried him off to safety.

"You can let go now," called out one of the birds.

"Are you kidding?" yelled the bear. "There's teeth on the other end."

Suddenly, Shere Khan spun about, and knocked Baloo onto his back with one powerful blow. The bear landed with a thud just as a flash of lightning lit up the jungle. Thunder boomed and another streak of lightning crashed into a nearby tree, which started to burn. Shere Khan drew back in terror and let out a roar.

"Fire!" squawked the vultures. "It's the only thing Old Stripes is afraid of."

The vultures carried Mowgli over to the tree and dropped low enough for him to grab a burning branch. Then they set him lightly on the ground.

Mowgli now had a weapon that could save Baloo's life. He started toward the tiger, who was about to slash Baloo with his mighty claws.

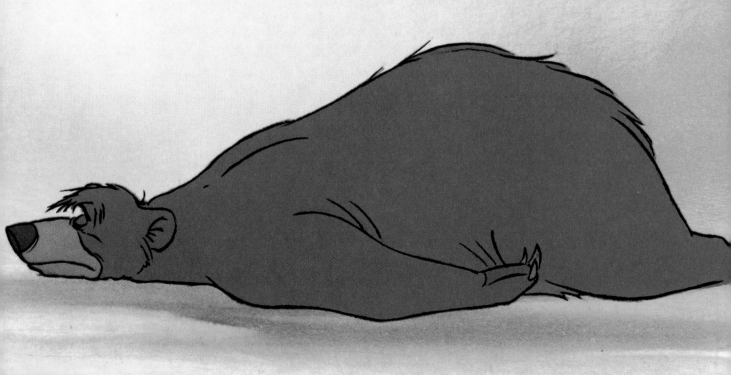

Shere Khan turned to watch Mowgli approach.

"This time, Man-cub, you won't escape," growled the tiger, starting toward him. He didn't get far. The vultures swooped down on him. One pulled his whiskers. "Stay out of my way, you mangy fools," roared Shere Khan. "I'll tear you to pieces."

While the enraged tiger swiped at the circling vultures, Mowgli carried out his plan. He tied the burning branch to Shere Khan's tail.

A terrified scream filled the jungle as the tiger raced away, the burning branch bouncing behind him.

"Well, that's the last we'll see of him," croaked one of the vultures.

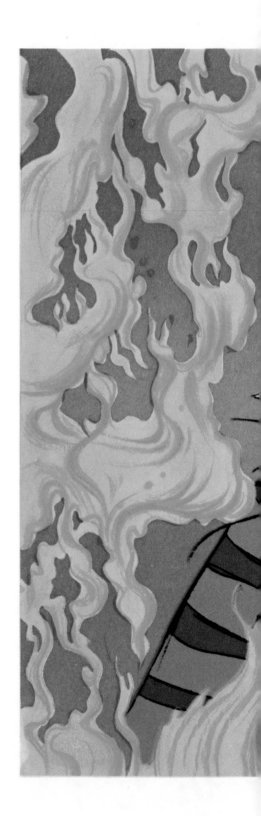

Bagheera finally caught up to
Baloo and Mowgli.

Mowgli ran to Baloo and knelt
beside him. "Wake up," he said,
shaking his friend. "Why don't
you wake up?"

At that moment, one eye
opened and Baloo sat up,
rubbing his head. The other eye
was swollen shut.

"Boy, I really showed that
tiger," said Baloo.

"I guess you did," Bagheera
said, "with a little help from
this Man-cub."

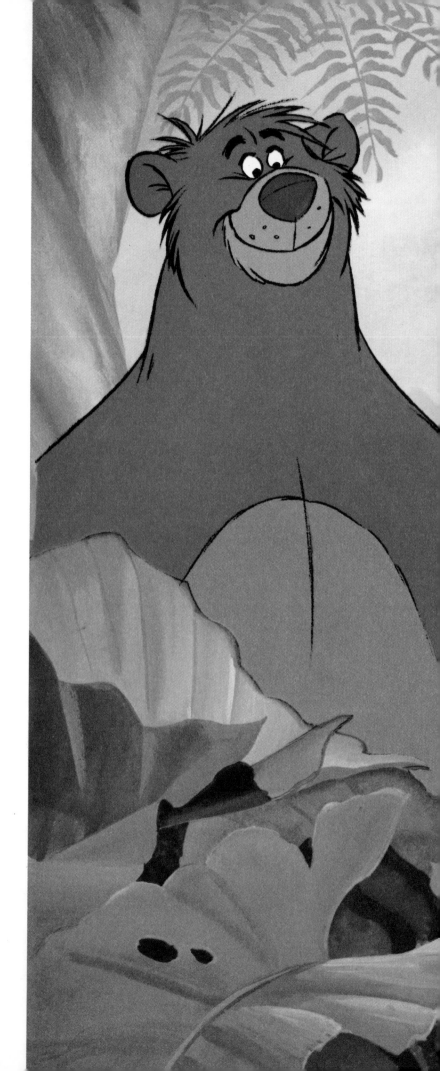

The next morning they went
down to the river for a drink.
As they drew near, Mowgli
heard singing. "What's that
sound?" he asked. "I've never
heard that before."

"Oh, that's nothing," said
Baloo, trying to start a little
sparring with his boxing
partner. But the Mancub wasn't
paying any attention.

Mowgli crept closer to the singing. He parted the branches and saw a young girl coming down to the river to get some water.

"Bagheera, what's that?" asked Mowgli.

"Oh, it's the Man village," he answered.

"No, not that," said Mowgli. "I mean *that*." And he pointed to the girl. "I've never seen one before."

"Go ahead, Mowgli!" Bagheera said. "Go have a closer look."

Mowgli climbed into a tree
overhead as the girl knelt at the
water's edge. She looked at her
reflection and then at one that
surprised her. It was a boy in
the tree up above. At that
moment, the branch broke, and
Mowgli fell into the water
beside her.

The girl giggled and smiled at him. Then she lifted her
water jug and Mowgli offered to help. He put it on his head as
he got out of the water. In a trance, he followed her back to
the village. From time to time, she stopped and smiled back
at him over her shoulder.

"It was bound to happen," Bagheera said as he and Baloo watched Mowgli walk into the Man village. "Now Mowgli is where he belongs."

"I guess you're right," Baloo agreed, "but I still think he'd make one swell bear." Then they went back to the jungle where they belonged.

ISBN 1-57082-040-6
10 9 8 7 6 5 4 3 2 1